For my brother
Britta Teckentrup

First published in hardback in Great Britain in 2013 by Boxer Books Limited.
This paperback edition first published in Great Britain in 2015 by Boxer Books Limited.
www.boxerbooks.com
Boxer® is a registered trademark of Boxer Books Limited.
Text and illustrations copyright © 2013 Britta Teckentrup
The right of Britta Teckentrup to be identified as the author and illustrator of this work
has been asserted by her in accordance with the Copyright, Designs and Patents Act, 1988.

A CIP Catalogue record for this book is available from The British Library

ISBN 978-1-910126-27-1

1 3 5 7 9 10 8 6 4 2

Printed in China

The art for Clumsy Duck was prepared by hand-printing paper
that was scanned and manipulated into a digital form.

All of our papers are sourced from managed forests and renewable resources.

# Clumsy Duck

### Britta Teckentrup

Boxer Books

Clumsy Duck was very clumsy.
She had just fallen over . . . again!
Not a day went by without her
stumbling, tripping or falling.
It was very frustrating!

"Hi there!" said Chick.
"Did you fall down?"
"Yes," said Clumsy Duck, "I did.
Why do I have to be so clumsy?"
"Don't worry," said Chick.
"Let's go for a walk together."

Duck and Chick went up the hill – twice!
The first time, Clumsy Duck tripped over a stone

The second time, Clumsy Duck bumped into a tree.

Finally they reached the top of the hill.
"What a wonderful view," said Clumsy Duck.

They set off along the muddy path.
Then, with a *slip, squidge, splat,*
Clumsy Duck splashed down in the mud!

"Oh, quack!" said Clumsy Duck.

Chick couldn't help a little chuckle.

"Come on," he said gently.

"Let's go to the pond and get you cleaned up!"

Clumsy Duck was worried.

Were her feet really that enormous?

Was there anything she could do?

Clumsy Duck and Chick waddled

and hopped along, not saying a word.

"Wow!" said Chick. "Look at your footprints. They're enormous! No wonder you are falling over all the time."

When they reached the pond,
Clumsy Duck asked,
"Why are my feet so big?"

"I don't know," answered Chick,
"but I'm sure there's a good reason.
Let's try and find out."

"Hmmm," mumbled Chick,
"maybe you can run really fast.
Come on, catch me."
Clumsy Duck chased after him.

She could waddle a lot faster
than she thought.
Until—*flump*!
"Never mind," said Chick.
"Let's try something else."

"Your big feet might be good for perching on a branch," said Chick.

Chick showed Duck how it was done.

Clumsy Duck jumped up too.

But her feet couldn't get a grip.

Poor Clumsy Duck fell off.

"Never mind," said Chick.

"Let's try something else."

"Maybe your feet are good for hopping," said Chick. Chick was good at hopping and hopped onto a large flat stone next to the pond.

"Copy me, Duck!"

But Clumsy Duck was not good at hopping!
She tripped, slipped and then splashed
into the pond.

Chick stared at Clumsy Duck in amazement.
"Look at you!" squealed Chick.
"You're the fastest, bestest, most elegant
swimmer I've ever seen."

And it was true.

Clumsy Duck was not clumsy in the pond.

She moved across the water like a ballerina.

"That's it, Duck!" cried Chick.
"Your feet are perfect for swimming!
If I could swim like you, I wouldn't mind
being clumsy on land!"
Duck was happily gliding around the pond.

And from that day on, Duck didn't mind one little bit that she was a clumsy duck on land because she was such a wonderful swimmer in the water!

# More Britta Teckentrup stories to enjoy.

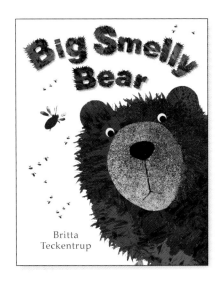

## Big Smelly Bear

When Big Smelly Bear gets an itch he cannot reach, Big Fluffy Bear offers to help him out. But first, she tells him, he must take a bath. A warm story of friendship with a sweet-smelling ending.

Paperback ISBN: 978-1-905417-43-8
Board Book ISBN: 978-1-907967-64-1

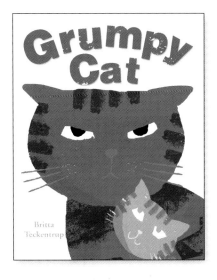

## Grumpy Cat

Cat eats, sleeps and spends his days alone. The other cats think he is a grumpy cat, but really–hc is just a lonely cat. But that is all about to change.

"Teckentrup has excellent control of the dynamics . . .
a tale that communicates perfectly the simple joy of breaking down barriers and letting people in . . ."
*Books for Keeps*

Paperback ISBN: 978-1-905417-70-4

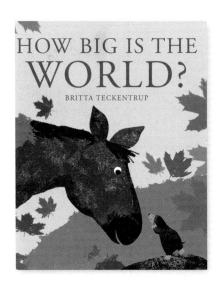

## How Big is the World?

Journey to the far corners of the world with Little Mole, as he travels from the frozen north to the tropics and asks the question, "How big is the world?"

"Large, vibrantly coloured double spreads and an absorbing story help make this an imagination-stretching picture book."
*Books for Keeps*

Paperback ISBN: 978-1-905417-62-9

www.boxerbooks.com